This book belongs to:

....

for all the
day-dreamers
of this
WORLD X

Henry Holt and Company, *Publishers since 1866*
Henry Holt® is a registered trademark of Macmillan Publishing Group, LLC
175 Fifth Avenue, New York, NY 10010
mackids.com

MOON RIVER will be published in the United Kingdom in 2018.
This edition is published by arrangement with Oxford University Press.
"Moon River" Words by Henry Mancini and Johnny Mercer © 1960.
Reproduced by permission of Sony / ATV Harmony, London W1FD.
Illustrations copyright © 2018 by Tim Hopgood.
This edition is published by arrangement with Oxford University Press.
All rights reserved.

Library of Congress Control Number: 2018936455
ISBN 978-1-250-15900-7

Our books may be purchased in bulk for promotional, educational, or business
use. Please contact your local bookseller or the Macmillan Corporate and
Premium Sales Department at (800) 221-7945 ext. 5442 or by e-mail at
MacmillanSpecialMarkets@macmillan.com.

First published in 2018 by Oxford University Press
First American edition, 2018
Printed in China by Leo Paper Group, Gulao Town, Guangdong Province
1 3 5 7 9 10 8 6 4 2

PICTURES BY
tim hopgood

MOON RIVER

BASED ON THE SONG BY JOHNNY MERCER & HENRY MANCINI

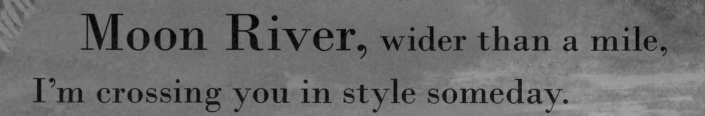

Moon River, wider than a mile,
I'm crossing you in style someday.

Oh, **dream maker,** you heartbreaker,

wherever you're going, I'm going your way.

Two drifters,

off to see the world.

There's such a **lot of world** to see.

We're after the same

rainbow's end . . .

. . . waiting 'round the bend,

my **huckleberry** friend,
Moon River and me.

Moon River,
wider than a mile,

I'm crossing you
in style someday.

Oh, dream maker,

you heartbreaker,

I'm going your way.

Two drifters,

off to see the world.

There's such a lot

of world to see.

We're

after

the

same

rainbow's end . . .

. . . waiting 'round
the bend,

my **huckleberry** friend,

Moon River and me.

MOON RIVER

BASED ON THE SONG BY
JOHNNY MERCER & HENRY MANCINI

Moon River, wider than a mile,
I'm crossing you in style someday.

Oh, dream maker, you heartbreaker,
wherever you're going, I'm going your way.

Two drifters, off to see the world.
There's such a lot of world to see.

We're after the same rainbow's end,
waiting 'round the bend,
my huckleberry friend, Moon River and me.

Moon River, wider than a mile,
I'm crossing you in style someday.

Oh, dream maker, you heartbreaker,
wherever you're going, I'm going your way.

Two drifters, off to see the world.
There's such a lot of world to see.

We're after the same rainbow's end,
waiting 'round the bend,
my huckleberry friend, Moon River and me.

I can't think of a better song to drift off to sleep to than "Moon River." It's a song full of adventure and big dreams. Stepping out into the unknown can seem scary, but instead of fear there is a powerful sense of hope running through the song, like the wide river itself, which keeps on flowing.

The joy of discovering new places and meeting new faces helps us to look at the world with fresh eyes. As we make our way through life, it's the friendships we make and the dreams we share along the way that make life's journey so worthwhile.

Sweet dreams.

tímhopgood